Mouseling's WORDS

STORY BY Shutta Crum
PICTURES BY Ryan O'Rourke

CLARION BOOKS   Houghton Mifflin Harcourt   Boston   New York

CLARION BOOKS
3 Park Avenue
New York, New York 10016

Clarion Books is an imprint of Houghton Mifflin Harcourt Publishing Company.

www.hmhco.com

The illustrations in this book were done in digital media.
The text was set in McKenna Handletter.

Library of Congress Cataloging-in-Publication Data
Names: Crum, Shutta, author. | O'Rourke, Ryan, illustrator.
Title: Mouseling's words / Shutta Crum ; illustrated by Ryan O'Rourke.
Description: Boston ; New York : Clarion Books, Houghton Mifflin Harcourt, [2017] |
Summary: A young mouse ventures out of the family nest to find the greatest
adventure of all: reading.
Identifiers: LCCN 2015024992 | ISBN 9780544302167 (hardcover)
Subjects: | CYAC: Mice—Fiction. | Reading—Fiction.
Classification: LCC PZ7.C888288 Mo 2016 | DDC [E]—dc23

Manufactured in China
SCP 10 9 8 7 6 5 4 3 2 1
4500671575

To my teachers at Dublin Elementary School—
thank you for opening my eyes to the worlds
within books. —S.C.

For Kaylee, Riley, and Liam. —R.O.

EVERY EVENING, I woke up surrounded by words. Aunt Tillie collected them from the Swashbuckler Restaurant, where words were SPECIALS OF THE DAY. Then she brought them to my family's nest—along with bits of food.

"*Noodles,*" I said as I pulled a scrap of paper from the nest. Aunt Tillie had shown me how to say it by puckering up my mouth. She'd taught all of us mouselings to read.

GRAPE SODA

YUMMY

if ZEST

TOMATO SOUP

I loved our nest, where I could touch words and whisper the ones I knew as I snuggled with my family. But one by one, my brothers and sisters left to find their own homes, their own paths.

"Come with me," the last one said. "It will be exciting!"

I looked at the words around me, at the soft, safe darkness of our nest, and shook my head.

Now I was the only mouseling at home.

One evening, Father folded his arms and heaved a big sigh. "You need to get a job," he said.

I ducked under a word that Aunt Tillie had recently brought us. "No! I'm too little."

Mother pointed to the passageway through the walls. "You need to find your path in the world," she said.

I glanced at the passageway; it did look a *bit* inviting. But I shut my eyes and clung to the nest. "No! I can't leave my words."

JUMBO BRAND

TOOTHPICKS

SWEET

TRA

Waffle

Aunt Tillie came. "You know, the world beyond this nest, beyond the restaurant, is full of words," she said. "You could go—"

"No-o-o! . . . What?" I sat up, and bits of nest slipped off my head. "There are words out there, beyond the restaurant?"

"Lots of them," Aunt Tillie said.

I plucked a word from the pile: IF. I stared at it. What *if* there were words waiting for me to discover them? What *if* they were even more special than the restaurant's special words?

I had to find out!

Mother packed a satchel for me with some bread and some of my favorite parts of the nest. Father settled his old fedora on my head. And Aunt Tillie winked and handed me a map with an X on it labeled HOME.

Beyond the outline of our building was an open space with a picture of a beast.

"What is *that?*" I asked.

"It's a cat," Aunt Tillie said. "I put it there to remind you to be careful out in the world."

"So I have to beware of beasts . . . like . . . like cats?" I shivered.

Then Father said, "Be brave!" And he scooted me toward the passageway.

Mother said, "Keep your paws clean and come home when you can. Oh, and here's some rope. Rope is always handy."

Aunt Tillie said, "Have adventures!"

Adventures with . . . cats? *Gulp!* Still, new words awaited me, and I wanted them.

I took one step, then two. I took a long look back.
Finally, I journeyed onward.

I saw a new world. And a word tumbled by!
What was it?

I glanced around. No cat. My heart was racing, but I darted out of our building and caught that word!

I traced the graceful lines of the mysterious word with my paw. I sounded it out, as Aunt Tillie had taught me. "S-i-i-i-n-n-n-g." Then I put the sounds together and said it quickly. "Sing!" It made my ears tingle. And I knew what it meant. Mother used to sing to us at bedtime.

I'd figured it out by myself!

I followed my map home and gave the word to Mother. She put it on display.

"It's a right treasure. Sounds good too," Father said. "Great work!"

Then and there, I decided that discovering words would be my job.

Just before dawn the next day, I ran across the open space and entered a quiet building. Inside, there were stacks and rows of blocky things and signs with words I didn't know, like LIBRARY and BOOKS. Then I spied another word. Its middle looked like two plump mouse bellies. Using my rope, I swung up and blew at the word until it drifted down, down . . . *oops!*

It landed on something large, something fast asleep. A cat! He seemed very much at home in the building. Perhaps it *was* his home.

I should have run away. But, *oh!* I ached to own that splendid, big-bellied word. Carefully, I slid down the rope until I hung so close to the cat's head that his ears tickled me. I leaned over, snatched up that word, and I was gone.

It was mine!

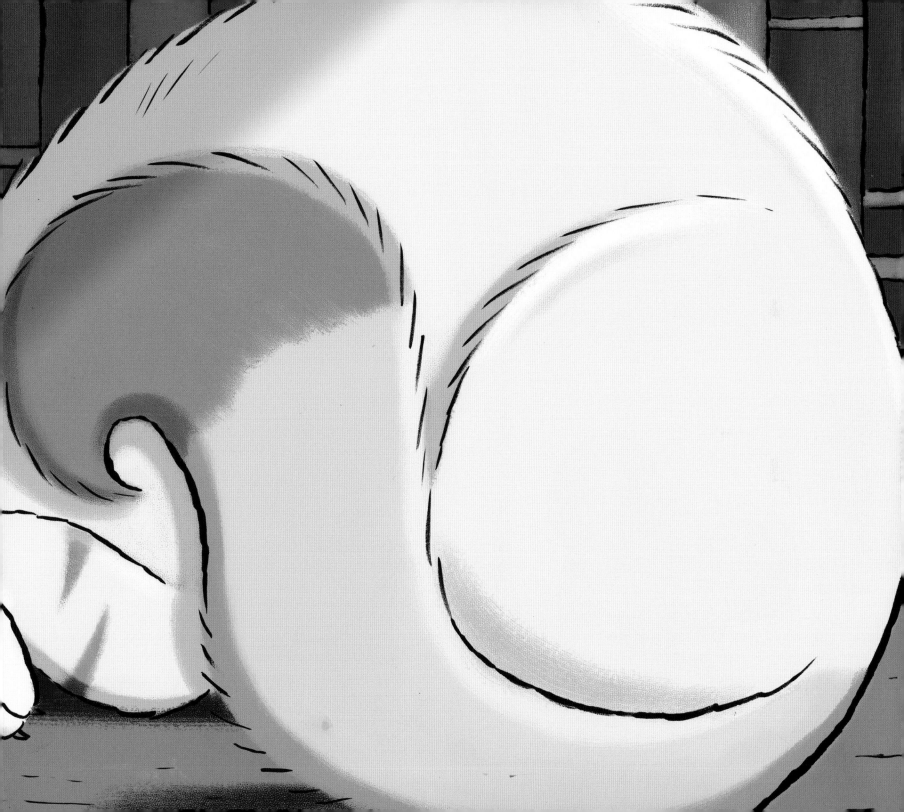

My parents gasped as I told them of my adventure. I laughed and held my prize aloft. *"Fl-o-a-t,"* I said, shaping my mouth around the word's middle.

"It's a word our customers enjoy," Aunt Tillie remarked. "Sometimes there are other words with it, like *ice cream*."

And so, like the daring explorer of Aunt Tillie's restaurant, I grew bold. I became a swashbuckler of words.

I climbed. I rappelled. I tunneled. I risked heart and snout to collect NIBBLE, WOW, and PERFUME— which smelled wonderful!

My favorite word was FUR. When I said it,
I could feel its softness whir in my throat.
I used my finds to build my own nest.

One time, I discovered a crinkly word. I was tiptoeing with it behind the sleeping cat when I tripped and fell!
Uh-oh.

The cat turned and stared. He twitched. Quickly, I mashed that word into a ball, drew back, and threw it at him!

The cat pounced on it. Then batted it with his paw. I laughed—*yes!* And I scampered off.

Later, I was nibbling on a milky word when a heavy paw slapped down on my tail. Caught!

I thought of all the undiscovered words that would never be mine. I thought of my family. I sniffed back a sob—and smelled my tasty new word. *Hmmm. Maybe the cat would prefer tasting it instead of me.* I staggered as I lifted the wet word above me, offering it to him.

He licked the word, and it slipped from my grasp. When he turned to lick it again, I ran! Behind me, a thrumming sound rattled my bones.

Purrrrrr . . .

On my next visit to the building, the cat was waiting for me. He jumped up and cornered me on a shelf. I no longer had a yummy word to offer him. Was he going to eat me?

He stretched out a paw—and swiped at one of the blocky things beside us.

What was this? Words—so many, many words! My head spun. My knees wobbled. I stumbled forward. Were there words inside *all* these things I'd climbed upon?

Yes! I . . . I never knew.

Running to one of the thick ropes
that bound the lion, the little mouse
gnawed it until it frayed and parted,
and soon the great beast was free.

"You laughed when I said I would
repay you," said the mouse. "Now
you see that even a mouse can help
a lion."

A kindness is never wasted.

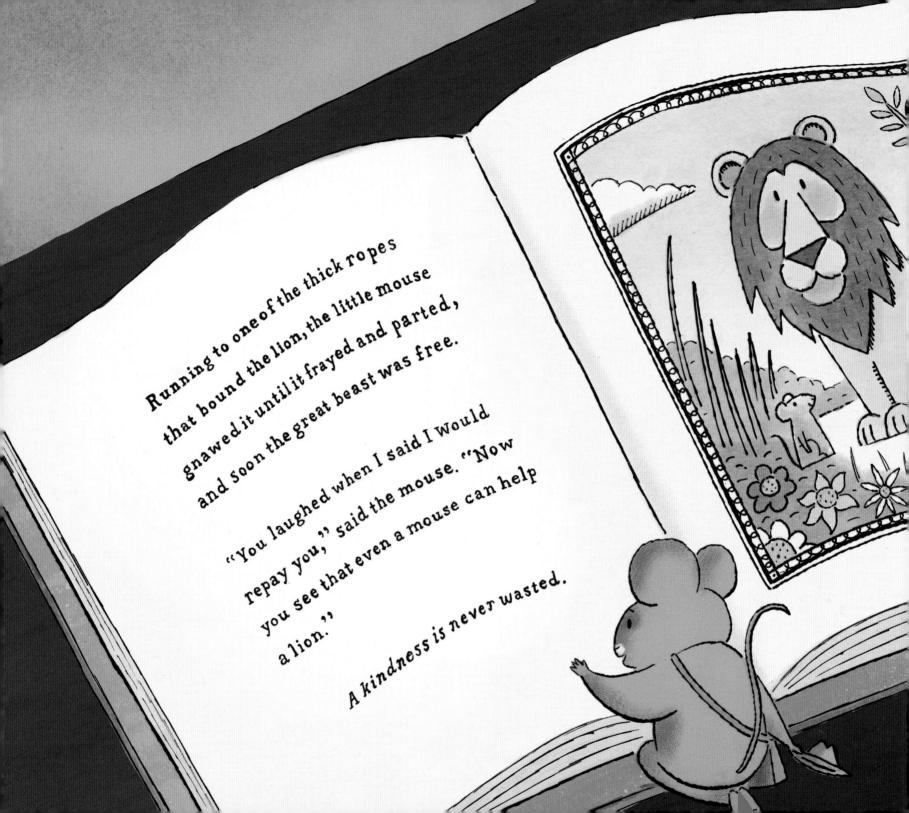

I took off my hat and knelt. My heart danced with happiness. Then I looked up at the cat.

He placed a paw gently on the field of words and looked at me. I understood. He was *not* going to eat me. He was waiting for something.

I looked back at the gift he had given me. What could I give him in return?

The best gift of all. I read a story to him.